DAY BY DAY WITH...

MILEY CYRUS

BY
AMIE JANE LEAVITT

Mitchell Lane

PUBLISHERS

P.O. Box 196
Hockessin, Delaware 19707
Visit us on the web: www.mitchelllane.com
Comments? email us:
mitchelllane@mitchelllane.com

Printing   1   2   3   4   5   6   7   8   9

RANDY'S CORNER

DAY BY DAY WITH. . .

Beyoncé
LeBron James
Miley Cyrus
Taylor Swift

Library of Congress Cataloging-in-Publication Data
Leavitt, Amie Jane.
  Day by day with Miley Cyrus / By Amie Jane Leavitt.
    p. cm. — (Randy's corner)
  Includes bibliographical references and index.
  ISBN 978-1-58415-856-1 (library bound)
 1. Cyrus, Miley, 1992—Juvenile literature. 2. Singers—United States—Biography—Juvenile literature. 3. Television actors and actresses—United States—Juvenile literature. I. Title.
  ML3930.C98L42 2011
  782.42164092--dc22
  [B]
                                                                    2010006528

ABOUT THE AUTHOR: Amie Jane Leavitt is the author of more than thirty books for children as well as numerous magazine articles, stories, activities, and puzzles. She graduated from Brigham Young University as an education major and prior to her writing career worked as a teacher at a private boarding school. She is an adventurer who loves to travel the globe in search of interesting story ideas and beautiful places to capture in photos. For this book, she'd like to thank her friend, Don Osmond, Jr., who gave her the inside scoop of what the daily life of a performer is really like.

PUBLISHER'S NOTE: The following story has been thoroughly researched, and to the best of our knowledge represents a true story. While every possible effort has been made to ensure accuracy, the publisher will not assume liability for damages caused by inaccuracies in the data and makes no warranty on the accuracy of the information contained herein. This story has not been authorized or endorsed by Miley Cyrus.

PLB

DAY BY DAY WITH

MILEY CYRUS

Miley Cyrus is an international superstar singer. She is also the star of the Disney Channel show *Hannah Montana*. Her days are very busy.

In the mornings, Miley does schoolwork. She doesn't go to a regular school, but she still has to study. Instead of a teacher, she has a private tutor. Miley reads books, does math problems, and studies history and science. After doing her homework, she goes to the television studio to rehearse her next show for *Hannah Montana.*

Before the show is taped, stylists fix Miley's hair, makeup, and nails. Miley has a lot of fun with her costars, including Jason Earles (left) and her dad, Billy Ray Cyrus.

Taping a television show is hard work. Sometimes Miley forgets her lines and laughs when she shouldn't. When this happens, they have to start over.

Miley gets a lot of support from her family. Her mom, Tish, and little sister, Noah, often travel with her on the tour bus. Sometimes her dad will travel with her, too, and sing a few songs with her onstage. Another plus: Miley even gets to bring her pets on the bus!

MOM

DAD

NOAH

11

12

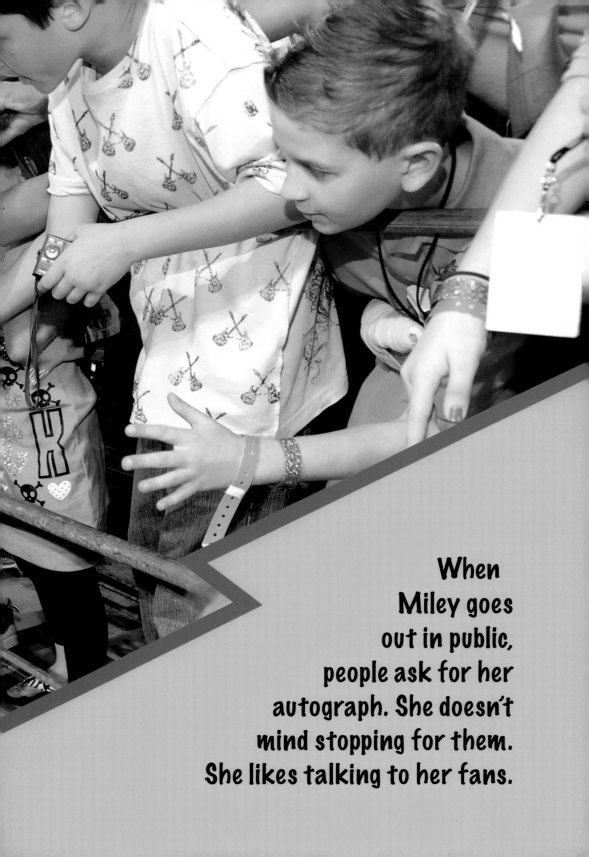

When Miley goes out in public, people ask for her autograph. She doesn't mind stopping for them. She likes talking to her fans.

By early afternoon, Miley is tired. Just think how much she has done already in her day!

She relaxes by checking her e-mail, texting her friends, and hanging out with her family.

Sometimes she and a few friends will grab milk shakes or go shopping for clothes, one of Miley's favorite activities.

17

Miley has made many friends as a celebrity. She and fellow singer Demi Lovato, who also has a show on the Disney Channel, are good friends.

They don't get to hang out very often, because they work on different sets, but they love it when they do get to spend time together.

Miley is also friends with the Jonas Brothers. She has performed with them in concert, and she and Nick Jonas (right) have become very close.

Miley believes in helping others. She goes to events that earn money for people and important causes. She also performs at benefit concerts.

FANS

the **ultimate** Mi party

PRESENTED BY
mileyworld.com

ON THE ROAD WITH

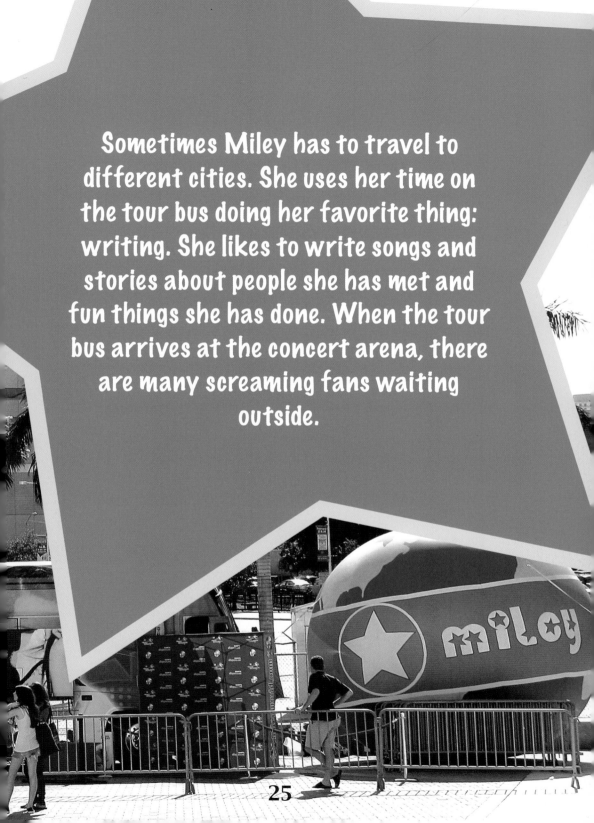

Sometimes Miley has to travel to different cities. She uses her time on the tour bus doing her favorite thing: writing. She likes to write songs and stories about people she has met and fun things she has done. When the tour bus arrives at the concert arena, there are many screaming fans waiting outside.

In her dressing room, Miley pulls on a sparkly costume, slips on high heels, and clasps her glittery jewelry.

She pictures the performance she's about to give.

When Miley runs out onstage, the crowd goes wild. She sings music from *Hannah Montana* and some of the songs she has written herself. Miley loves performing for her fans.

Smiley Miley has won many awards for her work in acting and music. Besides her show *Hannah Montana,* she has acted in *Hannah Montana: The Movie* and *Bolt.* With many more projects on the way, Miley's future is bright as day.

FURTHER READING

Works Consulted

Author interview with Don Osmond, Jr., April 25, 2009.

"5 Things You Don't Know About Miley Cyrus." *Newsweek,* February 11, 2008, p. 63.

Lewis, Kristin. "Miley Mania!" *Scholastic Scope.* November 10, 2008, pp. 24–25.

"Miley Answers Your Questions." *USA Today.* January 30, 2008.

"Jonas Brothers Launch Tour with Guests Miley Cyrus, Jordin Sparks," *Rolling Stone,* June 22, 2009. http://www.rollingstone.com/rockdaily/index.php/2009/06/22/jonas-brothers-launch-tour-with-guests-miley-cyrus-jordin-sparks/

Osmond, Donny. "Miley Cyrus." *Time,* April 23, 2008. http://www.time.com/time/specials/2007/article/0,28804,1733748_1733752_1734628,00.html

People, August 6, 2008. Miley Cyrus Special Issue, Vol. 70.
"At Home with Miley," pp. 26–29.
"Behind the Scenes of Hannah Montana," p. 48.
"The Many Sides of Miley," pp. 8–10.
"Miley Loves Pets," p. 36.
"My Doodle Diary," p. 73.
"My Favorite Things," p. 46.
"The Scoop on the Cyrus Siblings," p. 31.

On the Internet

Miley Cyrus Official Website http://www.mileycyrus.com/official

MileyWorld — Miley Cyrus Official Fan Club http://www.mileyworld.com/

INDEX